HELP FOR
MR. PEALE

STORY AND PICTURES BY

BARBARA MORROW

Macmillan Publishing Company New York • Collier Macmillan Publishers London

Macmillan Publishing Company
866 Third Avenue, New York, NY 10022
Collier Macmillan Canada, Inc.
Printed and bound in Hong Kong
First American Edition

10 9 8 7 6 5 4 3 2 1

The text of this book is set in 13 point Clarendon Light.
The illustrations are rendered in watercolor and pencil.

Library of Congress Cataloging-in-Publication Data
Morrow, Barbara. Help for Mr. Peale/
story and pictures by Barbara Morrow.   p.   cm.
Summary: With the help of his son Rubens, the famous painter
Charles Willson Peale finds a way to transport his natural history
treasures to a new museum in Philadelphia's Philosophical Hall.
ISBN 0-02-767590-4
1. Peale, Charles Willson, 1741–1827 — Juvenile fiction.
[1. Peale, Charles Willson, 1741–1827 — Fiction.
2. Natural history museums — Fiction.] I. Title.
PZ7.M84535He 1990 [E] — dc20
89–39273 CIP AC

To

ALAN

and

TOM

For all ten years of his life—from 1784 to 1794—Rubens had shared his home with the people of Philadelphia, who bought tickets to see the sights inside. They stood respectfully before the portraits of great Americans. They examined carefully the stuffed birds and beasts. And they marveled at the skill of Rubens' father, Charles Willson Peale, who had made the paintings and preserved the works of nature.

But now Father was taking his museum apart. Everything was to be packed up and moved to the family's new quarters in Philosophical Hall, six blocks away. Father himself was crating his precious paintings.

Rubens and his brothers were helping. Rembrandt was removing the stuffed animals from the handmade caves and the make-believe ponds.

Titian was packing the displays of insects.

Raphaelle was lifting the stuffed birds from their glass cases and from the arrangements of tree branches.

Rubens' mother, Betsy, and his little sister, Sophonisba, were overseeing the packing of the fine china.

Nimble-fingered Moses Williams was wrapping the huge, mysterious bones.

And Rubens was busy in the garden, caging some of the live animals and collecting in baskets the rare plants he had grown from seed.

Never had Rubens seen so many crates and cases, barrels and boxes. Towers of them grew in every room. "Father," he said, "how can we ever move all of this?"

"I thought I would hire men with carts to move the boxes," said Father. "But, oh, dear, I'm not sure about these!"

He was looking at the great stuffed American buffalo and the stuffed white-headed eagle. And he was considering the opposum and her babies, fixed to a tree limb, and the stuffed black bear, rearing on his hind legs, and the fox, and the water birds, and the rabbit, and... "Oh, dear," he said. "What shall we do?"

Rubens returned to work in the garden, and while he was moving a potted geranium, he had an idea. It made him grin.

"Father!" he called from below his father's window. "I know what to do!"

As Mr. Peale listened to Rubens' plan, he, too, began to grin. "Oh, splendid, splendid, my boy," he said. "You ought to begin at once."

So Rubens started off. Along the street, around the block, in and out of back gardens, up and down front steps he raced.

To every boy he could find, he whispered a message from the famous Mr. Peale.

On moving day, Father was pleased to see
a crowd of boys gathered in his garden.
"Boys," he said, "are you ready for the
parade?"

Of course they were! So Father arranged the procession that would wind from Third and Lombard streets to the new home at Fifth and Chestnut.

Father suffered much worry for the safety of his
treasures and was often out of breath from hurrying
back and forth along the route.

But, thanks to Rubens, everything except one small
alligator arrived safely at Philosophical Hall.

There, in time, with the help of Rubens and Raphaelle, Rembrandt, Titian, Mother, Moses, and Sophonisba, all was put to rights again. Then up went the sign over the door: MUSEUM. And the people flocked to see the sights inside.